SUPER CATS V

DR SPECS

GWYNETH REES

SUPER CATS V

DR SPECS

Illustrated by
BECKA MOOR

BLOOMSBURY
CHILDREN'S BOOKS
LONDON OXFORD NEW YORK NEW DELHI SYDNEY

BLOOMSBURY CHILDREN'S BOOKS
Bloomsbury Publishing Plc
50 Bedford Square, London WC1B 3DP, UK

BLOOMSBURY, BLOOMSBURY CHILDREN'S BOOKS and the
Diana logo are trademarks of Bloomsbury Publishing Plc

First published in Great Britain in 2020 by Bloomsbury Publishing Plc

Text copyright © Gwyneth Rees, 2020
Illustrations copyright © Becka Moor, 2020

Gwyneth Rees and Becka Moor have asserted their rights under the Copyright, Designs
and Patents Act, 1988, to be identified as Author and Illustrator of this work

A catalogue record for this book is available from the British Library

ISBN: PB: 978-1-4088-9425-5; eBook: 978-1-4088-9426-2

2 4 6 8 10 9 7 5 3 1

Printed and bound in Great Britain by CPI Group (UK) Ltd, Croydon CR0 4YY

MIX
Paper from
responsible sources
FSC® C020471

To find out more about our authors and books visit www.bloomsbury.com
and sign up for our newsletters

To my mother, Evelyn,

with love

CHAPTER ONE

A PURR-FECTLY CRIMINAL CAT

Tagg and Sugarfoot heard the theme music coming from the television and grinned at each other. Their whiskers shot forward excitedly as they raced to join the other cats at Super Cat Headquarters, who were all jostling for position in front of the large TV screen.

Tiffany Fluffiface was the most famous

cat on human TV (her cat-food commercials were legendary), and she had just started her own TV chat show, called *Cat Chat*, that aired after all the humans had gone to bed. Alongside Tagg and Sugarfoot, all the cats at Super Cat HQ were now glued to the screen, even the leader of their organisation – Topaz Top Cat!

'The subject I want to discuss on the show today, fellow felines,' Tiffany announced, her beautifully groomed fluffy tail swaying elegantly as she addressed the camera, 'is that of SUPER CATS! Super cats are cats with hidden powers! They might be able to fly or become invisible, they might have superior strength or lightning speed. But one of the big questions we're asking today is — are they *good* or are they *bad*? And do we need them or would we be better off without them? Today's guest is someone who has a very strong opinion on the subject ... so please welcome ... the brave ... the clever ... the ingenious ... the braintastic ... DR SPECS!'

The camera swung over to Dr Specs, a skinny, long-legged black cat with a circular white patch around each eye, which gave him the appearance of wearing human glasses. He swaggered confidently across the studio and sat on the low sofa next to Tiffany.

Tagg and Sugarfoot stared at the screen, dumbstruck! Dr Specs was the criminal who had recently escaped from Cat's End Prison.

They had been pursuing him for weeks with little success. They could hardly believe he was now brazenly appearing on television.

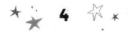

'Topaz!' Tagg exclaimed. 'Should we leave now and capture him at the TV studio?'

Topaz narrowed her eyes and leaned closer to the television screen. 'Let's see what he has to say for himself first,' she replied, as Tiffany started the interview.

'Dr Specs ...' Tiffany began in her purriest voice, 'do tell our viewers all about yourself.'

'Well, Tiffany, I am first and foremost a scientist and an inventor – the most ingenious cat inventor who ever existed, if I say so myself!' He gave a little laugh. 'I've spent my life inventing things that are useful to a cat who wants that little bit of extra security and power! I've made exploding cat crunchies, spyware disguised as fleas, collars with state-of-the-art weaponry sewn in, false teeth that release blood to fake your own death and escape your enemies.'

'Fascinating! And how did your work lead you to become involved with super cats?' Tiffany asked.

'Well, I used to work for Topaz Top Cat, the head of the Super Cat Organisation, but it soon became very clear to me that she didn't like my inventions. You see, these cats don't want ordinary cats to be on an equal footing with super cats.'

'Really? So are you saying the super cats felt threatened by all your marvellous inventions? Are you saying they *want* us to remain powerless?'

'Exactly, Tiffany.'

'And yet many of us imagine that super cats only want to *help* ordinary cats. Could

we have got that wrong?' She paused to give the camera a serious look. 'So, Dr Specs, can you tell us why *you* believe super cats are so dangerous?'

Dr Specs leaned in towards the camera, his whiskers shooting forward and his eyes becoming slits as he hissed, 'Fellow cats, what you need to know is that *super cats* – with their special superfeline abilities – cannot be trusted! All too often that power goes to their heads and they use their abilities for evil! SUPER CATS are the biggest threat to us ordinary cats! And I have PROOF!'

Suddenly the picture on the screen changed to footage of a terrible thunderstorm, and Tiffany Fluffiface's voice could be heard saying, 'This was the scene just a few weeks ago in the seaside town of Cats Haven, when

super cats Maximus Fang and Gory Gus unleashed their powers of weather control and telekinesis.'

The footage faded, and back in the studio Tiffany was speaking into the camera again. 'One cat who was badly injured in this storm, and whose home and mouse-catching business were totally destroyed, is here with us now. Mr Sniffer, please tell us what happened to you.'

'Good morning, Tiffany,' miaowed a croaky voice, as the camera panned to a one-eyed, scrawny-looking moggy who was now seated on the sofa between Tiffany and Specs. His head was bandaged and both front paws were in plaster. 'All I can say is that I have never been so terrified in all my life. At first I thought it was just a particularly bad

thunderstorm, but then the roof was ripped straight off my house!'

'Oh my goodness!' exclaimed Tiffany. 'Of course that would be terrifying for anyone.'

'Then I saw two cats in the sky, one with purple rays coming out of his eyes, and the other controlling the lightning as if he was a conductor and the weather was his orchestra!'

'Oh my!' gasped Tiffany. 'And they would be the infamous Gory Gus and Maximus Fang?'

'The very same! And let me just say that these cats were out of control! They didn't care who they harmed or what damage they caused!'

'So how were they stopped?'

'Well, even the other super cats couldn't stop them! The only way was to remove their powers completely and neutralise them – and a jolly good thing too!'

'It was my neutralising weapon that stopped Maximus Fang and Gory Gus from destroying the world,' Specs added crisply. 'But instead of thanking me by releasing me from prison, Topaz and the other super cats stole my weapon and kept me locked up. Well, now I'm free and I am campaigning for equality for all cats. Let us have no more super cats! We just don't know what they'll do next with their powers. I have already started building more weapons that will be available to ordinary cats, so they can protect themselves against super cats in the future. In fact these cats are not "super" at all. They only create havoc and are secretly intent on destroying our world as we know it!'

'Hear, hear!' agreed Mr Sniffer enthus-
iastically. 'I think all super cats should be
neutralised. Their powers must be disabled
so that they no longer pose a threat to the
rest of us.'

Tiffany stood up to shake paws with each
of her guests as they left the sofa. She then

turned to the camera.

'Well, that's all the time we have for today, *Chat* fans, but I'm sure you'll agree that was absolutely riveting. I'll certainly be getting a neutraliser as soon as I can. Join me next time for more *Cat Chat!*' Tiffany signed off with a swish of her tail as the theme music played, signalling the end of the show.

At Super Cat Headquarters, Topaz Top Cat turned from the screen to the other cats in the room, who all looked horrified.

'That evil criminal is trying to blacken our good name,' she mewed crossly.

Sugarfoot miaowed her agreement loudly. Tagg felt almost too queasy to mew. He was imagining what his life would be like without his superpower. It wasn't just that his power came in handy in difficult situations – his superpower was a part of him. Losing it would be like losing a part of himself. Without it he couldn't imagine even *feeling* like the same cat.

Tagg's older brother Rowdy growled, 'Do you think Specs is still at the television studio?'

'I don't know, but there's only one way to find out,' said Topaz. 'Tagg and Sugarfoot – go there and look for him.' She flexed her claws impatiently. 'Rowdy, you hold the fort here. I'm going to the lab.'

'Again?' Rowdy said with a frown. 'But don't you think we need to start planning—?'

'I need to supervise the scientists,' Topaz snapped. 'Call Marshmallow and get a backup team on standby.'

As they watched her go, Tagg asked, 'Is it true Topaz has hired more scientists to work on Dr Specs's neutralising weapon?'

'Yes. She's moved it from the lock-up to the lab. It's much less secure there, but she's obsessed with finding a way to reverse the neutralising effect. That's why she wouldn't destroy the weapon when we first captured it from Specs. And now she's so preoccupied with it, I think it's completely clouded her judgement!'

Tagg and Sugarfoot looked at each other. It was totally unlike Rowdy to criticise their boss and neither of them knew how to respond.

Rowdy suddenly switched into leader mode as he tapped Tagg impatiently on the shoulder. 'Why are you still here, agents? You already know what your mission is! Now GO! And remember to be careful. Dr Specs might not be a super cat, but we don't know what sneaky tricks he has ready to catch us out!'

CHAPTER TWO

TIFFANY FLUFFIFACE

'Wouldn't it be great if we found Dr Specs
and managed to capture him for Topaz?'
Tagg mewed as he and Sugarfoot slipped
through the gates into the TV studio where
Tiffany Fluffiface worked.

'Not just for Topaz,' Sugarfoot replied.
'Every super cat is in danger while he's free.
He's already making more weapons that can

take our superpowers away! We need to concentrate on following orders and getting the job done. No deviations or getting distracted!' She gave him a pointed look.

'Hey, I don't get distracted any more,' Tagg reminded her a little crossly.

'Sorry, you're right. That was the old you,' she teased. 'I'm just pulling your tail, Tagg! I know I never have to worry when I have you as my partner!' She gave him a proud grin. 'We make a great team. We can handle Dr Specs!'

They were in the part of the building where the dressing rooms were. A couple of humans emerged – probably famous ones – but Tagg and Sugarfoot were focused on looking for cats, and one in particular.

'I'll look around,' Tagg said. 'You wait here

and make sure Specs doesn't make a run for it.'

Even as he spoke, Tagg was disappearing into the background. His superpower — camouflage — meant that he could make himself virtually invisible by taking on the exact colours and scents of the environment he was in. It was the perfect superpower for a secret agent who needed to sneak around without being spotted.

Tagg flattened himself against the wall of the corridor to allow some more humans to pass by without tripping over him. He could faintly hear a cat's voice up ahead, so he hurried towards it, taking care to pad as quietly as possible. One thing he had learned as his superpower developed was that being camouflaged didn't dull the noises he made, and as cats' hearing was far superior to humans' he needed to be extra careful not to give himself away to either Tiffany or Dr Specs before he was in position.

As Tagg neared the dressing room where the cat's voice was coming from, he could hear that the miaow was that of a female – a rather cross and impatient one by the sound of it. It was the sort of miaow that cats tended to adopt when they were attempting to communicate with an extremely stupid human.

'It's lunchtime!' the cat was clearly yowling. 'And don't tell me cats don't need lunch, because this one does! Just a snack, mind you – I'm not Dr Specs! I've never seen anyone eat as much as he does at one sitting ...'

As a frazzled human hurried past, Tagg decamouflaged and entered the room, finding himself face to face with Tiffany Fluffiface herself. The long-haired Persian backed away from him instantly, as if she thought she might catch fleas. 'Who let you into my dressing room?' she snarled. 'SECURITY!!'

But the human security guards couldn't understand her and the feline ones – if there were any – seemed to be out of earshot.

'It's OK,' Tagg mewed quickly. 'I'm not here

to hurt you. I'm looking for Dr Specs. We saw him on your show. Is he still here?'

'Of course he's not still here! My show was recorded yesterday! And who's "we"?' Tiffany demanded snootily.

'I work for Topaz Top Cat. We're a team of super cats who—'

'I know all about Topaz. Dr Specs told me. She's the one who wrongly imprisoned him.'

'That's not true! He's actually a very dangerous criminal. He has to be stopped!'

'Stopped from saving the world from super cats?' Tiffany snorted.

'There are some bad super cats, but most of us are good!'

'Get out of here, before I throw you out!'

'Not until you tell me where to find Dr Specs,' Tagg mewed as he stood his ground.

'If you want to see him so much, then come to the rally we've organised for tonight! It's going to be massive!'

'A rally?' Tagg gasped. 'Where is it?'

'In the park – at the big wooden pavilion.

It starts at midnight. Dr Specs is going to speak, and I've organised some entertainment. We're going to film it all for my next show!' Tiffany grinned mischievously. 'Your presence should make for even more exciting viewing, but be warned! It's an ANTI-SUPER-CAT RALLY!'

CHAPTER THREE

THE ANTI-SUPER-CAT RALLY

The large ornate pavilion was located in a grassy area of the park where humans came during the day, but never at night. Tiffany's camera crew had been getting the lights and cameras in position, and now everything was set up ready for the rally.

After Tagg and Sugarfoot had returned to HQ to relay the new info, Topaz's team met to plan that night's operation. Rowdy was in charge, and several other cats with various useful superpowers – including Tagg and Sugarfoot – made up the rest of their unit on the ground. Rowdy's partner Marshmallow (who was still recovering from the broken leg he'd sustained in their previous mission) was their point of contact at Super Cat Headquarters. Normally Topaz was the one who coordinated everything from their base, but she hadn't wanted to leave the experiments on the neutralising weapon she was overseeing in the science lab.

The team's goal was to recapture Specs at the end of the entertainment, with as little commotion as possible. Several of the super-cat agents had hidden themselves in the bushes in the park, and Tagg was to use his camouflage to get as close as possible to their target once he appeared and make sure he kept him in sight the whole time. Dr Specs had evaded them too many times already since his escape from Cat's End Prison. Everyone was focused on capturing the cleverest and most menacing foe they'd encountered so far.

By midnight the grassy area was full of cats, for word had spread remarkably quickly about the event in the park. Tagg found it hard to believe that all the cats present were against super cats.

He understood how scary it must be if you were an ordinary cat at the mercy of a supervillain like Maximus Fang or Gory Gus. But he also knew that most cats thought super cats – Topaz's team in particular –

used their powers to help other cats and rescue them from dangerous situations.

So how had Dr Specs drawn such a huge crowd of anti-super-cat supporters? Unless ... judging from the One Purr banners that several groups of excited cats were waving, the popular cat band was the real reason for the large turnout. Tagg realised that One

Purr were the entertainment organised by Tiffany. Perhaps they didn't know what kind of rally they were performing at. In fact Tagg was almost certain that the band *couldn't* know since their drummer, Thumper, actually *was* a super cat.

So far there was no sign of Dr Specs. But Tagg kept his eyes glued to the stage.

Finally, after much impatient waiting, excited mews burst from the front of the crowd as Tiffany appeared onstage, a spotlight shining on her. Her shimmering coat sparkled like the stars in the night sky as she stood there, perfectly framed by the two magnificent white pillars of the grand pavilion.

'My fellow felines ...' she began, her rich, purry voice amplified by the microphone pinned to her long fur, 'please welcome my amazingly clever and inspiring guest ... Dr Specs! He is here to address you on a subject that is relevant to all of us – *super*-relevant, you might say!' She paused dramatically as cheers sounded from the audience, who were clearly in high spirits. 'And after that, the famous cat band One Purr is going to play for you!'

There were much louder cheers and catcalls and screeches of delight at the mention of One Purr, who were, after all, one of the top cat bands in the country.

'Tonight's event is being recorded for my next show,' Tiffany continued, 'so, everyone, please remember to smile for the cameras!'

The purring all around Tagg was deafening but he held his focus, waiting for Specs to appear. Had the villain spotted one of the super agents and guessed that they were waiting for him? Or maybe Tiffany had warned him they were coming. Though Tagg seriously doubted that Tiffany would have breathed a word to Specs – she was all about the sensational and wanted her TV show to be as exciting as possible. That was why she had invited the super cats. Their clash with

Dr Specs would make good TV – and all the better if Specs wasn't expecting them.

Although Tagg still couldn't see Dr Specs, he decided it was time to make his way to the pavilion. He hadn't reckoned on the crowd being so densely packed, though, and he found himself making slower progress than he'd anticipated. His camouflage meant that no one could *see* him, but they could certainly *feel* him as he trod on their toes and tails trying to get past.

'That's my tail you're stomping on, clumsy-paws!'

'That hurt, you fat fleabag!'

'Watch my toes, you big ginger lump!'

As he pushed his way through, cats on either side of him were spitting and hissing and accusing each other of shoving, and he moved as quickly as he could to stop a fight breaking out.

Tagg was extremely relieved when he finally arrived at the front of the crowd, just as Dr Specs appeared from the darkness behind the pavilion and leaped on to the stage.

Specs smiled confidently as Tiffany introduced him, then he stepped into the spotlight and began. 'Thank you and welcome to tonight's event, my dear felines. The title of my talk is "Super cats and their secret powers"!'

Specs delivered his speech with passion and conviction, easily appealing to the natural fears of all the ordinary cats in the audience. 'If we don't do something now, then someday soon these super cats will be the end of us all! We must act now! We must fight for our right to live in a normal world. All you parent cats out there, don't you want your kittens to be free to play in their own gardens without being terrified by a flying, invisible or super-speeding cat? And what about the truly evil super cats out there – like Maximus Fang, who caused catastrophe across the whole country? It was my weapon ... MY WEAPON ... that neutralised his power and saved us all from certain destruction!'

A few scrawny, angry-looking cats near Tagg began to chant, 'DOWN WITH SUPER CATS!'

Dr Specs continued in a creepy voice, 'Remember, I don't want to hurt these super cats – just *normalise* them. My weapon will restore these abnormal creatures to a normal feline state. And in doing so, I will restore order and peace to felines everywhere! It's only fair. It's only making us equals.'

A cheer went up, 'Hurrah for Dr Specs!' The cheer was soon echoed around the crowd – even the ones waving the One Purr banners.

Tagg felt a shudder of fear and was glad he

was safely camouflaged. Couldn't the other cats see that Dr Specs was dangerous?

Tagg checked out the area around the pavilion while Specs waved and joked with the crowd. Tiffany was standing in the shadows at one side, and on the grass behind the pavilion he could see the members of One Purr waiting for their cue to take to the stage. As soon as Specs was out of the spotlight, Tagg would signal for the other cat agents to move in and grab him.

As Tagg watched, Tiffany Fluffiface came forward to link front paws with Dr Specs as she announced, 'THEY'RE HERE, EVERY-ONE! THE CAT BAND YOU'VE ALL BEEN WAITING FOR! ONE PURR!'

As they all cheered, the cat musicians jumped on to the stage and Tagg immediately recognised Thumper, the long-haired ginger drummer. Thumper was a super cat, famous for his ability to shoot firebolts from his tail during his performances. His drums were made from shiny white animal skulls and his drumsticks were dog thigh bones. Tagg had seen the band play before, and he was struck by how uncomfortable their usually supercool drummer looked.

He guessed Thumper had been listening behind the scenes when Dr Specs had made his speech about super cats. He probably didn't want to be here at all now.

Dr Specs didn't leave the stage as Tagg thought he would, and was clearly visible standing at the side while One Purr played. Soon he was bopping away with Tiffany and the audience to the catchy opening number. That made him easy to keep an eye on.

'ONE PURR! ONE PURR! WE LOVE YOU, ONE PURR!' came the chant after the first song ended.

As the band launched into a much-loved ballad, which started off slow and then quickened in pace to the frenzied beat of Thumper's drums, the whole crowd joined in at the tops of their lungs. Everyone loved One Purr, and right now nobody seemed to care if their drummer was a super cat.

And that's when it happened!

It was One Purr's spectacular finale –

where Thumper pointed his tail and shot out his firebolts. Tonight, Tagg was close enough to the band to see how Thumper deliberately angled his tail to aim the bolts through the back exit of the pavilion so they would shoot safely up into the night sky.

Suddenly the stage lights went out. Only Tagg, from his position just across from Dr Specs, saw him rush forward and shove Thumper from behind. Thumper lost his footing, falling head first with his tail pointed straight up just as the first set of firebolts shot out. As the pavilion roof caught fire everyone screamed and poor Thumper toppled off the stage into the crowd, his tail firing automatically with fright, causing every cat in the audience to claw frantically at each other as they scrambled to escape.

Then Dr Specs's voice sounded clear and loud above all the din, 'THUMPER DID THIS! HE'S SET THE PLACE ON FIRE WITH HIS SUPERPOWER!'

Tiffany's cameras continued to film as pieces of the flaming roof fell down into the audience. Luckily all the waiting secret agents had sprung into action as soon as they saw what was happening. Using their super strength, super speed and other powers, they rescued injured cats and fetched bucketloads of water to hurl repeatedly at the flames.

Tagg was rushing to help when Sugarfoot called out to him. 'We have to catch Dr Specs! He's getting away! Look!'

Tagg turned to where she was pointing and saw that she was right. Dr Specs had left the pavilion and was slinking away in the dark across the grass. The only reason they could make out the mostly black cat at all was because Tiffany had turned up the spotlights to allow the rescuers to see what they were doing.

'He's heading for the south boundary,' Sugarfoot mewed. 'Come on! We have to follow him! There's no way he's going to escape from us this time!'

CHAPTER FOUR

DR SPECS'S EVIL LAIR

As Tagg was camouflaged and Sugarfoot was black apart from her single white paw, it was easy for them to follow Dr Specs without being spotted.

Dr Specs led them through various dark alleys until he stopped at a dilapidated building with boarded windows and a backyard full of discarded human objects –

a broken fridge, old chairs, a battered sofa. Specs glanced behind him before dodging past the sofa to the back door. The door had a hole at the bottom where the wood was cracked, and he swiftly disappeared inside.

As Tagg slunk past the fridge, he felt the ground move under his paws. Correction – his paws were sinking into the ground!

The earth seemed to be sucking him down. He was soon stuck fast!

'Stay back!' he yowled urgently to Sugarfoot. 'Don't come near me! I think it's quicksand! Specs must have set a trap in case he was followed.'

Just then the bulky fridge started to tilt towards him, until it was dangerously close to toppling over right on top of him.

'I'll deal with this!' Sugarfoot shouted, turning to face the fridge. She had a super yowl capable of hurling backwards anyone or anything in her path. Turned up a notch, her yowl could shatter any solid structure and send villains flying off into space.

With a mighty YOWL that shook the whole garden, she sent the broken chairs flying and the fridge falling backwards away from Tagg.

By the end of it, Tagg's entire coat was standing on end as if a giant hairdryer had just been aimed at it, and his paws had come unstuck with a loud squelch, sending gooey sand splattering everywhere.

Inspecting his muddy paws, Tagg forced himself not to stop and lick them but to lead the way into the house through the hole in the door. With Sugarfoot close behind him, they padded as softy as possible along a dark hallway.

'Be careful,' Sugarfoot whispered. 'He might've set more traps.'

They found themselves on a set of horribly creaky stairs as they climbed towards the light that was coming from the top landing. As Tagg trod on a stair near the top he got a very bad feeling and stopped abruptly, dropping his camouflage.

'What's wrong?' Sugarfoot hissed.

'It's this stair. It didn't creak.'

'That's because it's not a stair!' boomed a familiar Speccy voice, as the stair in question suddenly made a strange scraping noise. Tagg leaped backwards just in time as lots of sharp rotating nails pushed up through the wood to pierce the paws of any cat who'd been standing there.

A movement on the landing made the two

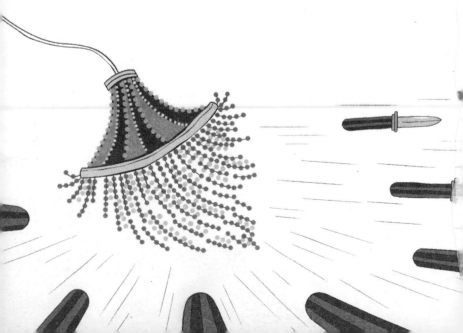

cats look up. Then there was a loud grating sound above them and a strange contraption swung down from the ceiling to hover overhead. It appeared to be some kind of chandelier that was dangling what looked like glinting daggers directly above them.

There was nothing for it but to run. As the chandelier swung across their escape route, showering its deadly daggers over the lower part of the staircase, Tagg leaped bravely upwards, right over the stair above them,

and yelled for Sugarfoot to follow. The chandelier was starting to swing back towards them as Sugarfoot made the jump and scrambled up the remaining steps and on to the landing. They flattened themselves against the back wall as more razor-sharp daggers hit the upper staircase and landing, one of them narrowly missing Tagg. The blade was so sharp it would have lopped off his tail if he hadn't swished it out of the way just in time.

Finally it was over and the house was silent again. They strained their ears to listen for further movement, but there was nothing, apart from their own quickened breathing.

No sound came from any of the rooms off the landing, though Dr Specs surely had to be inside one of them. The room that was closest had a dim light coming from it and the door had been left slightly open.

'He must be in there. I'll sneak in and look,' Tagg murmured, activating his camouflage.

'Be careful!'

Tagg crept into the room, just managing not to skid on a slippy patch on the floor. Looking down he saw that he was standing in some spilt cat food, while on the other side of the room Specs was gnawing at a ripped-open slippery sachet that kept escaping from under his nose. There was a dirty mattress with a pile of ragged blankets on top of it, a broken-looking stepladder, a few old pots of paint and some battered cardboard boxes. The light was coming from a strange sort of home-made flashlight perched in the middle of the floor, and Tagg wondered if Specs had invented it since it didn't look like any human contraption he had ever seen.

Tagg signalled to Sugarfoot that it was safe to enter – he couldn't *see* any more traps, at any rate – before he crept very slowly towards Dr Specs.

As soon as Dr Specs saw Sugarfoot come in through the door, he let out a little growl of annoyance. 'You're still alive?'

Sugarfoot blinked at him coldly.

'Still, at least I got rid of one of you! Tell me ... was it my home-made quicksand or my rotating nails that got him? Or did he make it as far as my Chandelier of Doom?' He chuckled.

Realising that Specs thought Tagg had

been eliminated, Sugarfoot kept up the pretence while Tagg moved closer. 'Topaz sent me here to arrest you! I'm taking you back to prison. Face it, you're no match for super cats.'

'Really?' The chuckle was gone in an instant as Specs snarled and showed his nasty yellow teeth. 'No match? If I robbed Topaz of *her* superpower, then don't you think I can easily do the same to you?!'

'Wait, *you* took Topaz's superpower?'

Sugarfoot blurted, unable to hide her shock at this revelation. Tagg also froze where he was.

'Of course I did! That's why she put me in prison! She couldn't bear that I was more powerful than her!' He let out a crazily gleeful miaow. 'You should have seen her face when I turned my weapon on her! She'd ordered me to destroy it! Can you imagine? *Destroy my ingenious invention?* I wanted to kill her, but I didn't! I just took away her power, with no serious side effects whatsoever! I should have been hailed a hero! I should have been crowned the best inventor the world has ever seen! But no – she flung me in prison to rot!'

Sugarfoot, who was struggling to control her emotions, murmured, 'What you did was wrong! Her superpower—'

'Shapeshifting into any animal she chose!'

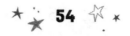

he exclaimed. 'It was a *spectacular* super-power!' He started to shake with mirth. 'But now she's nothing. And none of you can defeat me!'

Still camouflaged, Tagg was listening to all this, completely stunned. He remembered how, a long time ago, he'd asked his mother why the leader of the super cats wasn't actually a super cat herself, and his mother had started washing her paws and mumbled something about Topaz having been a super cat once and that he mustn't ask any more questions.

Dr Specs let out one last victorious laugh before suddenly jumping on to the mattress and diving under the pile of blankets.

'You can't hide in there,' Sugarfoot miaowed, still keen to bring this criminal to justice. 'You've nowhere else to go, Specs.'

'That's *Doctor* Specs to you!' came the growly reply, as the villain poked first his head and then the rest of his body out from the covers, revealing a familiar object clutched between his front paws.

'That's a neutralising weapon!' shouted Tagg, causing Dr Specs to jump with fright since he hadn't realised there was a second super cat in the room.

Specs quickly recovered and fired the weapon in the direction of Tagg's voice, but luckily Tagg had already darted away.

'GET BEHIND ME, TAGG!' Sugarfoot yelled, as she prepared to unleash her own superpower on Specs. But as the yowl emerged from her throat and the room began to tremble, Specs pointed his weapon and fired directly at her head.

'NO!' Tagg yelled, diving towards his friend and pushing her out of the way.

But it was too late. Sugarfoot fell to the floor, unconscious, and the room instantly stopped shaking.

'Phew! That little madam had me worried for a moment!' Dr Specs said with a chuckle. 'Now, what about her invisible friend? Though you're not *quite* invisible, are you?'

Tagg froze as Specs waved his weapon around the room, watching and listening intently for any indication of Tagg brushing against something or causing a floorboard to creak.

'Oh, well!' Dr Specs's teasing voice sang out, as he kept his weapon ready to shoot. 'While I wait for you to reveal yourself, I'll show you the best part of my plan. You can see how busy I've been while you've been chasing your own tails trying to capture me!' He sidled over to a large object covered in a dust sheet. He gripped a corner of the sheet with his teeth and whipped it off. 'Ta-da!'

Tagg only just managed to hold back a gasp as he took in the huge pile of weapons identical to the one Specs was holding. How could he have made so many so quickly? And how would anyone be able to stop him now? Tagg looked over at Sugarfoot, still unconscious. Had her power really gone?

'I intend to create my own army of cats,' Specs confided. 'So it shouldn't be too difficult to eradicate all super cats, don't you agree?'

Tagg felt trembly inside and it was hard to think clearly. His heart was beating furiously and he was scared Dr Specs would hear it. He had to stay calm if he was going to get himself and Sugarfoot out of here safely. He scanned the room for what seemed like forever, trying to think up a plan.

The one that came to him was risky, but it might work if he could manage to dim the strange flashlight. The dust sheet was lying on the floor by the window. Still camouflaged, Tagg carefully tiptoed towards it, before yanking it roughly with his teeth and throwing it over the flashlight. He leaped away as Specs fired at the sheet.

The room was dim and shadowy now as Tagg hurled an old paintbrush across to the other side of the room, where it clattered against the wall. As Specs turned to fire his weapon in the direction of the crash, Tagg rushed to Sugarfoot and began to pull her by the scruff of her neck towards the door. By the time Specs stopped firing, Tagg had dragged Sugarfoot out of the room and was already halfway down the stairs.

CHAPTER FIVE

A SCARILY
SILENT SUGARFOOT

Thankfully, soon after Tagg had got Sugarfoot out of Dr Specs's building, she recovered enough to stagger along beside him.

'Dr Specs is the most dangerous villain we've ever come across!' Tagg murmured in despair. 'And he isn't even a super cat!'

Sugarfoot tried to reply, but her throat hurt so much that she couldn't utter a single mew.

When they finally arrived back at Super Cat HQ, Topaz, Rowdy and Marshmallow were already there. Thankfully they had managed to control the fire in the park before any serious damage was done – though the humans weren't going to be happy when they saw the burned remains of their pavilion the next morning.

'Was anyone hurt?' Tagg asked.

'A few cats had minor burns but nothing too serious. We took them to the vet's house and left them with her. But what happened to you two?'

While Sugarfoot was helped to a comfy cat basket in the corner of the room, Tagg described their encounter with Dr Specs. 'He knows we'll go after him again, so he's bound to change his hideout. We'll have to go back straight away if we want to catch him!'

'I agree,' Topaz mewed. 'We need to get a team together quickly.'

But as they were about to make their plan, Topaz was distracted by one of the scientists who suddenly rushed into the room with a list of lab results. As she read it, her tail bushed up.

'What is it, Ma'am?' Rowdy asked urgently.

Topaz looked excited. 'I have to go back to our lab straight away. As you know, they've been working on Dr Specs's original weapon and they've just found something important. Rowdy, please take over here.'

'But, Ma'am, don't you think that capturing Specs is more important?' Rowdy began anxiously. 'He's made a huge pile of weapons already, and look what he just did to Sugarfoot.'

'My scientists are the only ones who can restore Sugarfoot's superpower,' Topaz mewed back. 'And mine,' she muttered to herself as she hurried away, her assistant scurrying behind her.

'Her priority should be catching Dr Specs before he distributes all those weapons,' Rowdy grumbled when Topaz had gone.

'She's not seeing the bigger picture,' Marshmallow agreed.

Tagg couldn't help feeling uncomfortable, knowing what he now did about Topaz's superpower and how Dr Specs had taken it from her.

From her basket in the corner, Sugarfoot tried to speak but found that it was too painful even to whisper. As she whimpered in distress, Tagg rushed over to her. 'You need to rest your vocal cords. If you do, then I'm sure your voice will come back soon.' At least, that was what he hoped.

Rowdy suggested they call Sugarfoot's parents, Flash and Glamour, to look after her while she recovered. 'Tagg, I need you to work with me and Marshmallow on a plan to stop Dr Specs.'

They had only just started their planning meeting – and Tagg was about to ask them if they already knew what Dr Specs had revealed about Topaz – when Flash arrived. Flash's power was super speed.

'Glamour is on her way,' he told them. 'So are Chester, Melody and Wild Bill. They should be here in a little while. We all want to help.' Chester and Melody were Tagg and Rowdy's parents. Along with Great-Uncle Bill, they were all retired super-cat agents who had once worked for Topaz. Perhaps semi-retired was a more accurate description, since they still lent a paw whenever the situation demanded it.

'Great. We need all the help we can get. Dr Specs is like no one we have faced before,' Rowdy grunted, as Flash hurried over to Sugarfoot.

The other cats in the agency gathered round to listen as Rowdy took Topaz's usual spot in the centre of the floor.

'Tonight has been a very bad night for super cats,' he began. 'Not only has Dr Specs created more neutralising weapons and fired one of them at Sugarfoot, but Thumper the drummer has used his superpower recklessly and caused a fire—'

'That fire wasn't Thumper's fault,' Tagg interrupted indignantly. 'He pointed his tail *away* from the pavilion. He was aiming to send the firebolts straight up into the sky. It was Dr Specs who shoved him forward so he fell off the stage into the audience.'

Furious miaows broke out and Rowdy had to call the meeting to order. 'Dr Specs must have got Tiffany to invite One Purr there on purpose,' he exclaimed. 'He *wanted* to use Thumper to make super cats look bad!'

'Where *is* Thumper?' Tagg asked.

'At the vet's. Tiffany stayed with him.'

'Tiffany?'

'She was really upset about the fire. And she was really angry with Dr Specs. I don't think she knew what he was going to do.'

Suddenly the door burst open and Topaz rushed into the meeting room. 'I have some important news!' she yowled. 'Our scientists have discovered that the weapon *does* have a reversal mode! But it can only be activated with Dr Specs's pawprint!

'I want him captured alive, and his paws must be untouched. They must not receive the slightest scratch, no matter what else happens! Is that clear?'

'Ma'am, of course we'll try, but if he comes at us we'll have to fight him off somehow. If I have to use my super strength to throw something at him, then—'

'I absolutely do not give you permission to harm his body in any way!' Topaz insisted.

'Unless the lives of the team are at risk, Ma'am ... that's the only time when we might have to forget about saving his paws.'

'Rowdy, under NO circumstances are his paws to be damaged!'

'But, Ma'am ...'

As the argument continued Tagg glanced at Sugarfoot, who was looking more and more upset, despite her dad's comforting presence.

Tagg tried to make himself heard above the loud miaowing of the other cats, but it was hopeless as Rowdy and Topaz's fiery discussion escalated. Topaz wanted to go in softly with a very small team, whereas Rowdy wanted to use every super cat they had, each of them fully prepared to use their superpower and do whatever it took to bring an end, once and for all, to the evil genius.

One thing was clear to Tagg – if they left it much longer, Dr Specs would escape again. Then there would be no chance of getting his pawprint *or* ridding the world of him and his evil plans.

That's when Tagg decided there was only one thing to be done, and while the others continued to argue, he slipped silently away.

CHAPTER SIX
TAGG GOES SOLO

It was starting to get light by the time Tagg reached Dr Specs's lair for the second time. He hadn't slept in a while, and for a few moments he felt as if he wasn't quite up to the task that lay ahead.

But then he gave himself a shake. Of course he was up to it! He was a super cat and one of Topaz's top agents, wasn't he? And just because he and Sugarfoot had always worked as a team on every mission until now, it didn't mean he wasn't capable of defeating their enemy on his own! He was sure that if their situations were reversed, Sugarfoot would be here right now, preparing to unleash her super yowl and do whatever else it took to defeat Dr Specs and save her friends!

Switching on his camouflage, Tagg gave the fridge and the other human junk a wide berth as he pushed through the hole in the back door, taking care to avoid brushing against the sharp, splintery wood.

Once inside, he paused for a moment to listen. Nothing. He couldn't tell whether Dr Specs was at home or not. Cautiously he climbed the stairs. He usually felt safe when he was camouflaged, but this time, against this particular villain, he did not.

He jumped over the hazardous stair and kept an eye out for any nasty surprises above his head. He reached the upstairs landing safely. Directly ahead was the door to the room they had entered before. As he stepped towards it he heard a creak to his left, then a muffled bang from the same direction, like a window shutting. Had Specs heard him coming and decided to make a quick exit?

Tagg moved swiftly to his left, where another door greeted him. It was slightly ajar and he stopped to listen. Hearing nothing, he nudged it open a little further with his nose, tentatively pushing his head through the opening.

This room seemed to contain several pieces of furniture covered with dust sheets. There was a window at the far end, which was closed. Tagg thought he smelt cat food, though there was no sign of Dr Specs.

As he tiptoed inside he spotted a movement behind one of the sheets. Instantly the door banged shut behind him and all the dust sheets fell to the floor at once, revealing various items of impressive-looking laboratory equipment. Coiled around this equipment were what looked like green garden hoses with large spray nozzles.

Before Tagg knew what was happening all the hoses switched on at the same time and he was hit from every angle, but not by water. The substance being sprayed at him was thick, oily paint!

From one side he was doused in red paint, from the other blue, from behind him yellow and from in front green. As the paint stuck to his fur, he gradually became visible, like a patchwork cat materialising bit by bit out of thin air. There was no escaping the cleverness of it – or the evil cackle of feline laughter that accompanied it.

'Call that camouflage a superpower?' Dr Specs spluttered scornfully. 'I don't even have to use my weapon to neutralise it! A few splashes of ordinary paint will do the trick! You have to be the most useless super cat I've ever met – and I've met quite a few!'

As Tagg rubbed the paint from his stinging eyes, he saw Dr Specs perched on top of a large crate, holding his belly as he shook with laughter. He was wearing some kind of weird padded jacket over his lab coat, but before Tagg could wonder what it was for, he felt a sharp pain cutting into his leg. One of his hind legs was caught in a snare.

'I set that little snare-trap just before you got here,' Dr Specs explained. 'Old-fashioned but effective. My exceptional brain thinks of everything, you see! I need you to stay put! Can't have you running around in my laboratory – you might break something!'

'*This* is your laboratory?' Tagg gasped. He had been expecting something with wooden benches and test tubes and Bunsen burners, possibly with a dissected mouse on display, which was silly, he realised, considering what it was that Dr Specs was manufacturing. 'What are all these ... these machines and things?' he asked.

'Oh, they're very high spec. Only the best scientists use them.' He began to point at the various pieces of expensive-looking equipment resting on tables around the room. 'That's my particle counter, that's my acid cleaner, that one's my magnetic analyser, and that's my high-density solidifier. Oh, and in that box,' he pointed to the crate he'd been perched on when Tagg arrived, 'are my fire extinguishers, just in case any of my experiments go wrong!' He chuckled. 'You see, it takes a lot of research to make a weapon as sophisticated as mine.'

'I don't understand,' Tagg spluttered. 'Why are you doing this? Why do you hate us so much?'

Dr Specs seemed to be considering this. 'Well, it's complicated, dear boy, though I

suppose we do have a little bit of time before
I kill you.'

'K-k-kill me? I thought your weapon only
took away our powers?'

'The first one did – the one I used on Topaz.
I thoroughly enjoyed that. I knew I was

getting rid of my chief rival, you see.'

Tagg didn't see. 'Chief rival for *what*?'

'My rival for ultimate power, of course! I want all cats to bow down to *me*! But first I need to eliminate all you other super cats. You see, I never get any of the credit. No one ever thinks I'm a hero! When your power is hidden inside you, like mine, nobody realises it *is* a superpower! Nobody calls it pure genius! Nobody invites you to go on TV to talk about it! No! They only want you to come and talk about all the *other* super cats out there!'

'Wait, you're saying, *you* have a superpower?'

'Of course I do! My genius is my superpower! How else do you think I came up with a way to invent a neutralising weapon? Do you really think an ordinary cat could be *that* clever?!'

As Tagg began to process this, Specs

continued. 'For years I felt hurt that my superpower wasn't recognised, but then I learned how to turn it to my advantage. I could pretend to be an ordinary cat and still use my power to get what I wanted. And now ordinary cats think I am their ally. They don't even realise I am making them do exactly what I want. Completely ingenious, wouldn't you say?'

Specs had moved closer to Tagg as he talked, and Tagg realised the boastful villain was almost within grabbing distance. If he could just reach out his front paws far enough to make contact … but then what would he do? It wasn't like he was super strong like Rowdy. Maybe Specs was right when he said Tagg's power was useless. He was starting to think he should never have come here alone.

Specs stepped closer and gave Tagg a massive shove to his chest that sent him reeling backwards.

The snare pulled even tighter around Tagg's leg, making him whimper.

Smirking, Specs bounded over to a cupboard, which he opened to reveal another stash of neutralising weapons, just like the one he had used on Sugarfoot.

'I've enjoyed our little conversation, Tagg,' Specs told him with a creepy laugh. 'Unfortunately, I've told you far too much to allow you to live. But the good news is, you're going to be the first cat to see my updated weapon in action when I switch on my brand-new "kill" mode.'

Tagg could do no more than remain a sitting target for Specs, who was making a big thing of getting himself in a comfortable position as he pointed the weapon directly at Tagg and adjusted one of the levers.

Tagg said nothing but gave him a cold stare, trying to convey all the hatred he felt in that last gaze.

'Oh, don't look so glum,' Dr Specs said with a grin. 'Look on the bright side – this way you won't have to worry about what you're going to do for the rest of your life without your superpower.'

And with a little chuckle he pulled back the lever, ready to fire.

CHAPTER SEVEN

TAGG SAVES THE DAY AND A PAW

There was a sudden gust of wind as something furry and blurry flew past Tagg at lightning speed. Dr Specs let out a screech as the weapon was whipped out of his paw!

'Flash!' Tagg cried out in relief.

Flash slowed to a halt, revealing the weapon clamped between his teeth.

Specs saw him and spat viciously before diving towards the cupboard of weapons. Flash was too quick for him though, pouncing on Specs and knocking him into a corner of the room.

'Are you OK, Tagg?' Flash shouted as he stood in front of the pile of weapons while Dr Specs shook with rage in the corner. 'Why are you covered in paint?'

'He did it to block my camouflage. My leg

is trapped too.' He gritted his teeth, not wanting to show how much pain he was in from the wire cutting into his back paw.

'Melody and Chester are on their way. They'll soon get you free,' Flash assured him.

'Flash, look out!'

Dr Specs was approaching them, carrying what looked like a large Christmas bauble between his teeth. It must have been hidden in the corner somewhere. He tossed the bauble at Tagg so that it landed right at his front feet. Tagg immediately spotted the sparkling fuse. It was a bomb!

'You idiot! You'll blow us all up!' Flash shouted, but the evil villain just laughed.

'Not me – just you!' he snorted. He turned scornfully to Tagg. 'You know, my boy, I almost feel sorry for you. It must be terrible to have such a rubbish superpower and no brains!' And with that he took a small remote out of his pocket and pressed the button. It controlled a panel in the roof, which slid back to reveal the cloudy night sky.

At the same time Dr Specs tugged at a bobble on his strange jacket and the back fell away to reveal a small jetpack concealed inside. 'I guess I'll see you around!' he called out. 'Bits of you anyway!' he added with a snigger. And before anyone could stop him he had rocketed up through the opening in the roof.

Flash rushed over to Tagg. 'Where's the

bomb? We have to get rid of it!'

Tagg was looking surprisingly calm. 'I tossed it back at him just before he launched himself. I *think* it went into his lab-coat pocket.'

Flash's jaw dropped open. He was speechless.

They both stared up through the hole in the roof, hardly able to believe that Dr Specs was about to be blown to smithereens by his own bomb.

'You said you *think* … ?' Flash murmured hoarsely.

'I'm *almost* certain,' Tagg murmured back.

At last, above their heads, the sky suddenly lit up with an explosion.

'Phew!' Tagg grunted, and both cats slumped to the floor in relief.

★ ★ ★

A few minutes later the other super cats arrived. First came Rowdy and Marshmallow pounding up the stairs, followed by Tagg's parents, Melody and Chester, and Sugarfoot's mother, Glamour.

Melody lost no time in using her super claws to cut through the wire snare and release Tagg. Then Glamour used her super lick to heal the nasty wound on his hind paw. Meanwhile, Flash explained what had happened and how Tagg had saved them with his super-quick thinking.

'That's amazing work, Tagg!' Chester told him. 'We're so proud of you!'

Rowdy stopped examining the cupboard of weapons and came over to give Tagg a lick. 'You've rid the world of a very evil cat. Well

done, little brother … I mean, Agent Tagg!'

'I couldn't have done it if Flash hadn't saved me when he did. How did you know where to find me, Flash?'

'Sugarfoot got her voice back – just a whisper but it was enough to tell us where she thought you'd gone.'

'Sugarfoot! I can't wait to see her and tell her that Specs is gone for good.'

'The trouble is, so is her superpower,' Rowdy said with a sigh as he stared up through the hole in the roof. 'And Topaz's.'

'But—'

'Don't worry, Tagg,' Rowdy added quickly. 'It couldn't be helped. I'll explain everything to Topaz.'

'But—'

'Rowdy's right,' Flash added. 'And

Sugarfoot would rather the two of us were alive, Tagg, even if she doesn't have her superpower.'

'Yes, I know that, but I have to show you something!' Tagg finally got the words out. 'We may not have Specs's paw, but we do have his paw*print*! Look!' He stood up and pointed to his chest. The green paint all over his front was now dry and in the centre of his chest they could see the pawprint Dr Specs had made when he'd shoved Tagg.

The others all stared at it. It certainly looked like a perfect copy of a cat's pawprint. But would it work as well as Dr Specs's actual paw?

Back at Headquarters, the scientists took Tagg into the lab, where they scanned the pawprint and ran various tests on it.

Tagg felt very nervous as he lay on his back on one of the tables while the scientist cats set the neutralising weapon on his chest, carefully positioning it so that the pawprint lined up with the right place on the weapon.

'Are you ready for this?' they asked Tagg. 'We've no idea what will happen.'

'Then let's find out,' Tagg miaowed bravely. In fact he was terrified that the weapon would suck out all *his* superpower too.

His power might not be as awesome as some other cats', but he couldn't imagine life without it. It was only because he knew that this was Sugarfoot's only chance to get her superpower back that he'd agreed to do it.

The scientists pressed the weapon firmly against the green pawprint on Tagg's chest. Then they waited.

Tagg felt the weapon become warm before it began to vibrate. His fear increased and all his instincts told him to jump off the table and run – then, from somewhere inside the weapon, came a muffled click. The scientist cats looked excited.

'Is that it?' Tagg asked nervously.

'Probably. But there's only one way to know for sure. We need to try it out on Topaz and Sugarfoot.'

It wasn't until Tagg heard the squeal of delight from Sugarfoot, followed by the rumble in her throat that always preceded a super yowl, that he was sure the pawprint had worked. Sugarfoot emerged from the lab, yowling in celebration. They had reversed the neutralising weapon!

'Sugarfoot, I'm so glad to have you back!' he declared, giving her the wettest lick ever. 'You *and* your super yowl!'

'You seemed to manage OK without us today,' Sugarfoot pointed out with a smile.

'Maybe, but I like it much better when we work as a team!'

Topaz emerged from the lab behind Sugarfoot, also looking happy, but said she wanted to be left alone for a while so that she could try out her superpower in private. It had been a long time since she'd used it and she was feeling unexpectedly emotional.

Meanwhile, the scientists were dispatched to Dr Specs's lair to supervise the destruction of the neutralising weapons, which were currently being guarded by Rowdy and several of their best agents. They were also going to find suitable homes for all the laboratory equipment.

The following day, when all the new weapons had been successfully destroyed and Dr Specs's lair had been sealed off, Topaz called a special meeting. Every agent was required to attend.

'I wonder if she's going to award you another medal, Tagg?' Sugarfoot said. 'You certainly deserve one!'

'Don't be silly!'

It turned out that Topaz did have a surprise for Tagg, although it wasn't a medal.

With all the super cats gathered around her in a circle, Topaz relayed her thanks to every cat involved in the mission. 'Tagg in particular has shown great skill and courage, and because of that I have recommended him for a special honour. He will be interviewed on television by Tiffany Fluffiface, who is eager to show her viewers that Dr Specs was completely wrong about super cats.'

'Tagg, that's amazing!' Sugarfoot purred.

'Television? ME?' Tagg exclaimed in disbelief.

'A TV star, eh? Better have a good long bath before then, Tagg!' Rowdy teased, because although Tagg had managed to rub off some of the paint, there were still lots of splotches on his fur.

But before Tagg could respond, Topaz had a further announcement, one which none of them was expecting ...

CHAPTER EIGHT

A CAT-TASTIC CONCLUSION

'Now that my superpower is restored, I can think clearly again,' Topaz told them. 'I can see how obsessed I've been about regaining my power, and how I've let that need come before the real mission. That's why I've decided it's time that I retired and made way for a new cat to lead you. The cat I am choosing as my successor is Rowdy. Do you all agree?'

'Rowdy!' A cheer went up. Clearly all the super cats thought he was the natural choice as their next leader.

'But what about you, Topaz?' Melody asked. 'What will you do?'

'I am going travelling. I shall go where I've always dreamed of going – to the jungle!'

'The *jungle*?!'

'Not in this form but in my new one.' With a flash of blue light, the small grey cat in front of them transformed into a huge graceful panther.

'WOW!' All the other cats backed away, not sure what to expect next.

But the panther was still Topaz. 'Panthers don't belong in this country, obviously, so I am about to embark on a long and exciting journey overseas,' she told them with a rich panthery purr. 'Though, of course, I won't be making the journey like this.'

With another blue flash, the huge panther disappeared and a blue-and-white swallow perched on the window ledge. 'Luckily it's almost migration season,' Topaz's voice came – a little squawkily – from the bird's beak. 'I just need to find some feathered companions to show me the way. Now if you'll just push the door open for me …'

Rowdy and Chester opened the door as wide as it would go, and then they all stood back to allow the beautiful bird to spread its wings and fly out. They followed it outside to watch as it soared away above the trees in the park, wings outstretched in the classical V-shape of the swallow.

'I think I understand now why she was so desperate to regain her superpower,' Rowdy murmured in awe. 'That has to be the best power of all.'

A few days later Tagg was back at the studio, preparing to go on Tiffany Fluffiface's TV show, where he was being billed as 'the cat world's newest hero'.

Sugarfoot had come with him to keep him company in the special room where Tiffany's guests waited before the show. It was called the Cream Room, which Tagg thought was an odd name until he saw the delicious refreshments Tiffany had provided for her feline guests.

'This is yummy,' Tagg said, licking the whipped cream off the top of his second

helping of liver pâté.

'Only the best for Tiffany's guests,' said the cat who had come to take him through to the studio. 'You're on in five. Do you mind licking that cream off your nose first?'

'I'll do it,' offered Sugarfoot, removing her head from a sardine trifle and rushing over to him. 'There! You look very handsome, Tagg! I'm so proud of you!'

Tagg began to wish that he hadn't eaten quite so much as he was led into the studio. He felt like he was about to burp. *How* many cats had Tiffany said would be watching him today? His parents would be glued to the TV for sure! What if he couldn't think of anything to say? He didn't want to look stupid!

'Here he is!' Tiffany's excited voice sounded as he stepped into the studio, where she awaited him on a plush velvet couch. 'Come and sit beside me, Agent Tagg ... Fellow cats out there, I want to introduce you to one of our finest cat heroes. Tagg is a crime-fighting super cat, and he's going to tell us how he recently foiled a plot that would have endangered all of us ... a plot hatched by one of the most evil and dangerous villains of our time. But before that, Tagg, I have one simple question – we know it can be dangerous at times ... but do you *enjoy* using your superpower to fight crime?'

Tagg felt his nerves vanish as he thought about just how much he loved his job. 'Yes, I do,' he replied. 'You see, I'm part of a team of amazing super cats, who all work together.'

And he found himself purring excitedly as he faced the camera, eager to tell every cat who was watching just how *miaow-vellous,* *cat-abulous* and *purr-fect* being a super cat was!

COULD YOUR PET BE

Take this quick quiz!

1. Does your pet mostly ...
a) Sleep?
b) Play?
c) Spend time outdoors?

2. What does your pet like doing most?
a) Sleeping
b) Trying out new things
c) Getting into mischief

3. Does your pet have lots of friends?
a) No, it's quite solitary
b) Maybe. Certainly lots of different animals visit our garden
c) Yes! So many I lose track

4. Have you ever seen your pet do something incredible?

a) Not really, they just sleep a lot

b) Once I thought they had completely disappeared, but when I looked again they were right there ...

c) Yes! My pet once ran out of the garden so fast it burst through the fence!

Mostly a – Your pet might have had superpowers once, but they have probably retired now, like Uncle Bill

Mostly b – Your pet could have superpowers ... keep watching to see if any develop

Mostly c – Your pet definitely has superpowers! Wow!

CHAPTER ONE

A PURR-FECTLY ORDINARY FAMILY OF FELINES

Tagg was born in the spring – the first of five tabby kittens born to his mother, Melody, and father, Chester. It was Melody's second litter and this time she had her kittens in the family wardrobe, on top of her human's cleanest and most comfortable sweater.

Melody and Chester were fairly laid back when it came to kitten-rearing. Melody prided

herself on being able to lick a kitten spotless in two minutes flat, and Chester didn't bat an eyelid if one of his offspring tried to climb a tree or went to investigate next-door's cat flap without asking. All kittens got into trouble, he said — especially the adventurous ones. They either learned from their mistakes, or they lost their nine lives rather quickly.

'I know that sounds harsh,' Melody told the kittens, 'but your father is right.

The sooner you realise how perilous the outside world can be, the sooner you will learn not to do stupid or dangerous things.'

Tagg, who was a handsome tabby kitten with a white tummy, white paws and a thick stripy tail, glanced shyly at his father. All the kittens were in awe of Chester – a huge stocky ginger cat with dark green eyes. 'Did you do any stupid or dangerous things when you were young, Dad?' he asked curiously.

'I don't believe I did many *stupid* things,' Chester replied. '*Dangerous* perhaps – at least for an ordinary cat.'

'What sort of dangerous things?' Tagg was so excited to hear more that he forgot to ask what his father meant by 'ordinary'.

'Nothing you need to know about at the moment,' Melody told him swiftly.

As the months passed, Tagg noticed that his parents were treating him differently to the other kittens. He wouldn't say he was their *favourite* exactly, but he was certainly the one they scolded and fussed over the most, and he was always the one Chester took hunting.

It wasn't long before Tagg knew far more than his siblings about the arts of catching

4

mice, stalking birds and correctly judging whether your prey would fit through the cat flap *before* you made a complete fool of yourself with a dead squirrel.

As Tagg approached six months of age, he was the only kitten of his litter still living with his parents, and it wasn't because no humans had wanted him. Twice Tagg had been rehomed to a new human household, and twice his parents had come that same night to retrieve him. Each time his father had carried him home by the scruff of his neck, until in the end their humans had given up and let him stay.

Tagg didn't really mind. He liked their comfortable home in its quiet, tree-lined street. He had a cat flap to come and go as he pleased, a plentiful supply of food and water

and a well-stocked fish pond in the garden (even if it was covered with an irritating metal mesh).

On his six-month birthday, Tagg was excited as he scampered out into the garden.

'Uncle Bill has caught a mouse for me to play with,' he called out to his parents, who were curled up together on the grass. Wild Bill, who was Tagg's great-uncle, lived on his own in the rickety summer house at the bottom of their garden.

'Wait, Tagg,' Chester said urgently. 'We need to talk to you.'

'Yes, Dad.' Tagg sat down obediently, hoping this wouldn't take too long. His great-uncle wasn't as sprightly as he used to be and Tagg was worried the elderly cat might not be able

to stop his gift from scampering away if he didn't get there quickly. That was if Wild Bill could manage to refrain from eating it. After all, it was no secret that he was extremely partial to a bit of fresh mouse.

'Now that you are six months old, we want to tell you something about our family,' Melody began. 'It's a secret you must never repeat to anyone. Do you understand?'

Tagg's ears pricked up immediately. He loved secrets. 'Of course, Mum.'

'Good.' She looked at Chester to continue.

'Although your mother and I may seem like ordinary cats,' Chester began, 'we both have a very special ability. A *super* ability, if you like.'

'Wow!' Tagg was even more excited. 'Do you mean you have super*powers*?' His mother

had often told him bedtime stories about cats with superpowers, but he had always assumed the adventures were made up.

'That is exactly what I mean,' Chester replied.

'Wow!' Tagg exclaimed again. 'So what can you do?' Maybe his mother and father could fly! Or turn invisible! That would explain how they were so good at creeping up on him whenever he was scratching at the carpet or stealing food from the kitchen table.

'Well ...' Chester sounded like he was making the most serious of announcements as he stated, 'your mother has extremely sharp claws.'

Tagg let out a spluttery mew of mirth. He couldn't help it.

Chester hissed. 'This is not a laughing matter!'

'Sorry.' Tagg struggled to get his face straight again as he stammered, 'It's just … well … surely … don't *all* cats have those?'

'Allow me to demonstrate,' Melody said with a twinkle in her eye as she lifted one of her paws and stretched out the digits. Her claws seemed to go blurry for a few moments, then, all of a sudden, they changed into curved blades that radiated an odd, gleaming energy. The miniature swords looked totally unreal on the ends of her dainty white paws.

'Yikes!' Tagg blurted out. 'I mean, that's … *awesome!*'

Melody turned around to face her kitten.

'My super claws will cut through anything, Tagg,' she said. 'And I mean *anything*.'

Tagg gulped. Looking nervously at his father, he asked, 'So what can you do, Dad?'

Chester crouched down on his back legs and began to swing his hindquarters like any cat preparing to spring. But then he leaped off the ground and up, up, up, as high as the roof of the house and right over it.

Tagg raced around to the front of the house as fast as he could, but by the time he got there his father had vanished. 'Where is he?' Tagg mewed in wonder as he searched the sky.

'Oh ... several streets away by now, I expect,' Melody replied as she joined him. 'His back legs are *extremely* powerful.' She gave Tagg's head a gentle lick. 'I know it's a lot to take in, but don't worry. You'll be used to the idea by the time your own power develops.'

'M-my own p-power ... ?' Tagg gasped.

'That's right. You might have super claws or super strength, or you may develop something completely different. Whatever your power is, your father and I will be here to teach you how to use it properly. That is why we couldn't let you leave us like your brothers and sisters.'

Tagg suddenly thought of something. 'But how come *I'm* the only one? What makes *me* so special?'

'Nobody knows why only one kitten in each litter is born with superpowers,' Melody explained. 'But I *knew* you were the one from the moment you were born.

It was exactly how I felt when your brother Rowdy was born. He was the super kitten from our first litter.'

'Rowdy?' It was the first time Tagg had heard the name. 'What superpower does he have? Where is he now?'

'He decided that he wanted to go off on his own and explore other places. He has super strength, like Chester.' Her voice was light but Tagg thought she looked sad. 'Now, didn't you say something about a mouse?'

'Oh yes ... wait ... does Uncle Bill know about this?'

'Of course. He's a super cat too – at least he *was*.'

'Really?' Tagg immediately thought of the impressive stench of cat wee in the summer house. His mother had told him that it was just as well Uncle Bill's wee was so powerful because it meant any strange cats steered well clear. Tagg asked uncertainly, 'So does he have super *wee*?'

Melody let out a little snort. 'Of course not. His wee is quite ordinary, believe it or not. There's nothing unusual about a male cat spraying his territory, though your uncle does take it a bit far. No ... Wild Bill had super *teeth*. They could bite through anything – glass, wood, metal, vets' instruments ... And if he clamped on to something – or some-body – there wasn't anything you could do to shake him loose!'

'Wow! That sounds *mega* awesome.'

'It was. Unfortunately, all his teeth have fallen out now and he has no superpower left. And speaking of Uncle Bill ...'

'I'd better go!' Tagg gasped, suddenly thinking of his promised mouse.

'Make sure you eat it all up afterwards, Tagg,' his mother reminded him. 'You know how I feel about cats who only *play* with their food.'

Tagg found his great-uncle sitting outside the summer-house door, thoroughly washing his whiskers.

'Oh no,' Tagg miaowed crossly. 'You've eaten it already, haven't you?'

The older cat looked up and gave him a calm blink. 'I most certainly have, young fella. Fresh mouse can be extremely hard to resist if you're that way inclined. That's why I told you to come straight away. Now off you go while I take my nap.' Wild Bill napped after every meal these days, saying that at his age he couldn't be expected to digest food *and* stay awake at the same time.

Looking at his great-uncle now, Tagg found it hard to believe that the elderly tabby cat with absent teeth and patchy fur had once been a super cat.

He couldn't keep the excitement from his voice as he blurted, 'Mum and Dad just told me about their superpowers!'

'Time you knew,' the older cat grunted matter-of-factly. 'So how does it feel to be the son of Feline Force One?'

'Feline Force One?' Tagg asked.

'That was their secret-agent code name. Of course, there were others – Feline Force Two, Feline Force Three, Feline Force Four and such like. Me – I always worked alone.

My code name was The Gnasher.' He gave a purr of pride.

'Wait – you were *secret agents*?' Tagg wondered what other information his parents had left out.

'That's right. Our boss, the top cat, was called Topaz. She lived at HH with the leader of the humans.'

'HH?' Tagg asked.

'Human Headquarters. It's in the middle of the biggest human city. Anyway, the top human at the time was a real cat lover and he often talked to Topaz about his worries. She learned about all the problems in this country, and that's how we got our missions. When a different human leader came into power, Topaz was prepared to stay and help her too, only this one was allergic to cats and she found herself banished.'

'That's terrible!'

'It certainly was. Topaz was forced to close down the whole operation. After that we moved here. Your parents had kittens and I lost my last few teeth.' He belched and Tagg caught a strong whiff of freshly devoured mouse.

'Mum told me about Rowdy,' Tagg said.

Wild Bill grunted. 'Too headstrong for his

own good, that one. Took off without a mew to anyone. Haven't heard from him for almost two summers now – goodness knows where he went.' Wild Bill yawned. 'Now ... if you don't mind, I've some serious sleeping to do.' And two minutes later Wild Bill was gently snoring.

GWYNETH REES

Gwyneth Rees is half Welsh and half English and
grew up in Scotland. She studied medicine and qualified
as a doctor before she became a full-time writer.
She lives near London with her husband,
two young daughters and one noisy cat.

BECKA MOOR

Becka Moor is a children's book illustrator and storyteller living in Manchester. You can find her illustrations in a variety of fiction books and series as well as picture books. She has an obsession with cats and loves anything a bit on the quirky side.